castaway
cats

For Ponder, who inspired me
—L. W.

For Lisa W.
—P. G.

Atheneum Books for Young Readers • An imprint of Simon & Schuster Children's Publishing Division • 1230 Avenue of the Americas • New York, New York 10020 • Text copyright © 2006 by Lisa Wheeler • Illustrations copyright © 2006 by Ponder Goembel • All rights reserved, including the right of reproduction in whole or in part in any form. • Book design by Abelardo Martínez • The text for this book is set in Golden Cockerel. • The illustrations for this book are rendered in acrylic paint and ink. • Manufactured in China • First Edition • 10 9 8 7 6 5 4 3 2 1 • Library of Congress Cataloging-in-Publication Data • Wheeler, Lisa, 1963– • Castaway cats / Lisa Wheeler ; illustrated by Ponder Goembel.— 1st ed. • p.   cm. • "A Richard Jackson Book." • Summary: Fifteen felines find themselves marooned on an island and are not sure what to do. • ISBN-13: 978-0-689-86232-8 • ISBN-10: 0-689-86232-6 • [1. Cats—Fiction. 2. Castaways—Fiction. 3. Islands—Fiction. 4. Cooperativeness—Fiction. 5. Stories in rhyme.] I. Goembel, Ponder, ill. II. Title. • PZ8.3.W5663Cas 2005 • [E]—dc22 • 2004000541

castaway
cats

story by Lisa Wheeler · art by Ponder Goembel

A Richard Jackson Book
Atheneum Books for Young Readers
New York London Toronto Sydney

On an island
in the ocean,
near the land of Singapore,
midst a storm of great proportion,
fifteen cats were washed ashore.

Water dripped from wilted whiskers.
Sea salt stung exotic eyes.
Fifteen felines felt quite fearful;
each had used up several lives.

There were seven scrawny kittens
and a Persian Blue named Flo.
A tough tom known as Mittens
was a shorthaired calico.

One tabby, looking shabby,
and a bobtail known as Link,
helped a soaking wet Angora,
who was sure her fur would shrink.

The tawny twins with toothy grins
were natives of Siam.
A marmalade stood up and said,
"I think we're in a jam."

"We need shelter," said the tabby,
as he led them to a cave.
Then the kittens started bawling,
until Mittens said, "Behave!"

Fifteen cats by tempest blown—
Seven babes and eight full grown.

In the morning,
as the sun rose,
fifteen cats rubbed sleepy eyes.
The grown-ups searched for breakfast
to appease the kittens' cries.

They drank milk from the coconuts.
The ocean teemed with fish.
A broken shell served each cat well
and made a humble dish.

"This is *purr*-fect," said Angora,
as she licked her lovely lips.
"Don't get cozy," said the tabby.
"It is time we looked for ships."

The twins climbed up the rocky cliff.
Each kitten took a tree.
Thirty eyes scanned the horizon
for a savior from the sea.

And although they kept their vigil,
and although they raised a flag,
and although they kept a watch fire . . .
fifteen hopes began to sag.

Fifteen cats me-yowl with woe—
Nine above and six below.

"No more waiting!" said the tabby,
and he firmly set his jowl.
"You are *not* the boss!" said Mittens.
The Angora said, "Meee-*ow*!"

"Don't get catty," warned the Persian,
  as she whipped her plush blue tail.
"We have to work together.
  We must build a boat and sail."

"Good idea," responded Mittens.
"We are not here on vacation."

  The marmalade stood up and said,
"What a sticky situation."

They scoured the shore for flotsam,
and for driftwood that would float.
They gathered vines for lashings,
and they tried to build a boat.

"Tie it this way!" said the tabby.
"Do it our way!" said the twins.
"Hurry! Hurry!" mewed the kittens,
as they raced to see who'd win.

Fifteen cats work by the sea.
Fifteen cats cannot agree.

Then Bobtail bumped the Persian,
and the twins just up and quit.
Angora chipped a painted claw
and threw a hissy fit.

"No time for spats and spouting,"
 said the shorthaired calico.
"We need more wood and palm leaves.
 Move your tails now. Go! Go! Go!"

But the cats would not get moving.
No, they wouldn't even try.
And they wouldn't work together . . .
so, the fur began to fly!

Fifteen cats lie on the shore—
Ten are bruised and five are sore.

In the evening,
as the moon rose,
fifteen cats rubbed achy jaws.
They hung their heads in silence,
as they licked their swollen paws.

"We are foolish," said the Persian,
as she wrapped her tattered tail.
"We *have* to work together,
for divided we will fail."

So they sat around the fire
and organized a plan.
Then early the next morning,
after breakfast . . .
they began.

"Let me help you," said the tabby.
"You're so thoughtful," said the twins.
"Look what we found!" mewed the kittens,
 as they toted empty tins.

Each feline helped another.
Each feline did his share.
Each feline worked till sunset.
Now the boat was nearly there.

Fifteen cats slump in a heap—
Two awake—thirteen asleep.

"It's so lovely," said the Persian
as she gazed out at the sea.
"The island feels like home now,
all you cats, like family.
When we get back to the mainland,
will each feline go his way?"

"I hope not," mumbled Mittens.
"All my life I've been a stray.
  I would miss these little mewlers."
Then he tucked the kittens in,
  as he struggled with a lonely sigh
and stroked each tiny chin.

The tabby sobbed agreement,
  as he rubbed a sleepy eye.
Angora woke, the bobtail choked,
  the twins began to cry.

One by one the kittens each
arose and added pleas.
"Can we stay?"
"Is there a way?"
"We never want to leave!"

"We're staying!" Mittens shouted,
joined by cheers of happy mews.
The marmalade woke up and said,
"I'll spread the lovely news!"

Fifteen cats by tempest blown.
Fifteen cats have made a home.